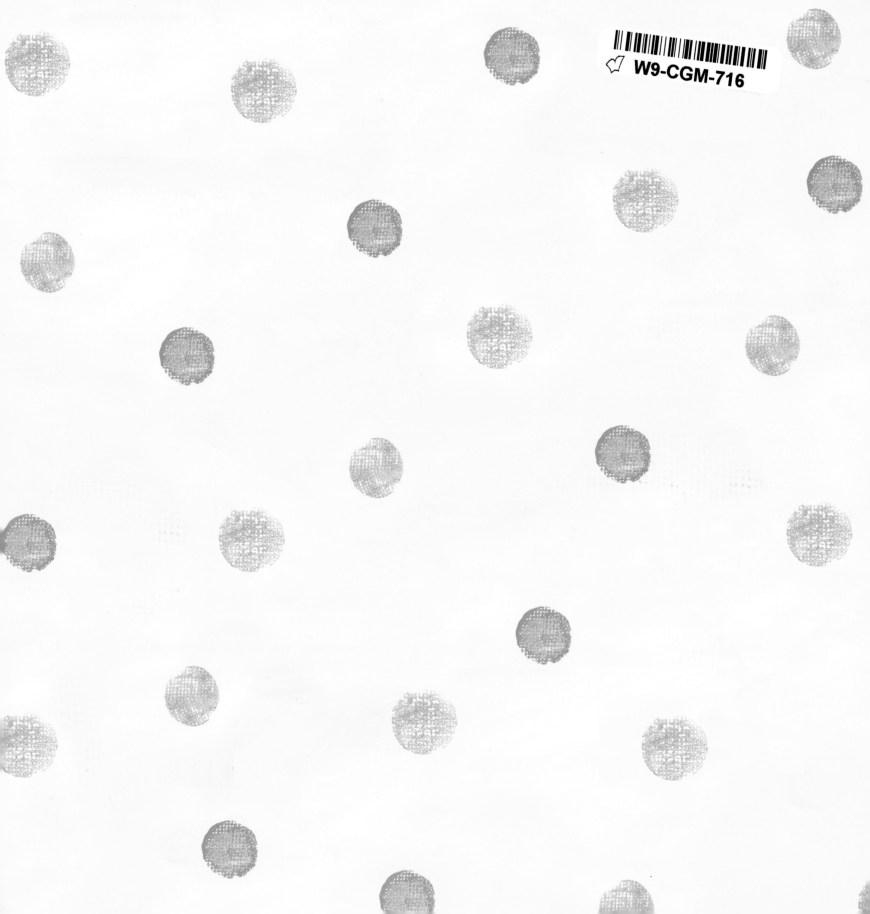

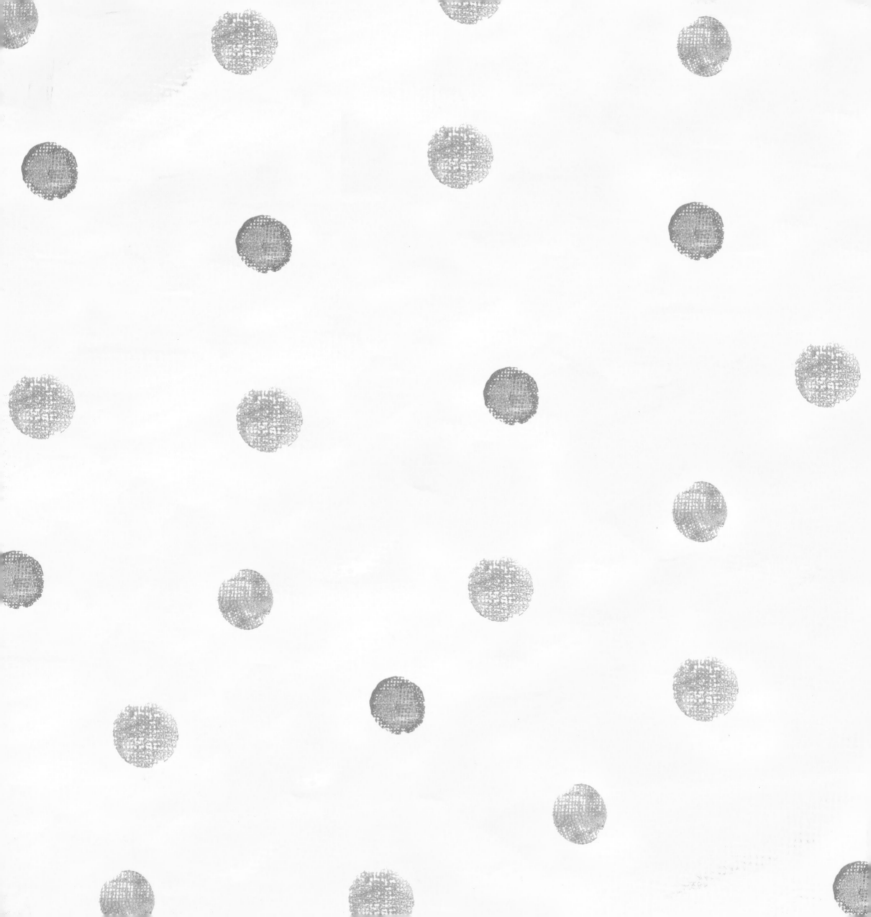

Fish Kisses and Gorilla Hugs

By Marianne Richmond

Fish KISSES and Gorilla HUGS

Library of Congress Control Number: 2006908876

Marianne Richmond Studios, Inc.
420 N. 5th Street, Suite 840
Minneapolis, MN 55401
www.mariannerichmond.com

ISBN 1-58209-807-7
This printing manufactured exclusively for Books are Fun®.

Illustrations by Marianne Richmond

Book design by Sara Dare Biscan

Printed in China

Second Printing

Also available from author & illustrator
Marianne Richmond:

The Gift of an Angel
The Gift of a Memory
Hooray for You!
The Gifts of Being Grand
I Love You So...
Dear Daughter
Dear Son
My Shoes Take Me Where I Want to Go
Dear Granddaughter
Dear Grandson

Plus, she now offers the *simply said...* and *smartly said...* mini book titles
for all occasions.

To learn more about Marianne's products,
please visit
www.mariannerichmond.com

Fish KISSES and Gorilla HUGS

Thanks, Adam, for making
bedtime so much fun
for everyone! — MR

RALPHIE brushed his teeth
and had three stories read.
But Ralphie Mix, at age of six,
didn't want to go to bed.

I'm wide awake! said Ralphie,
   and Mom, I see a bug
crawling 'cross the carpet
      and underneath my rug.

I don't think so, Ralphie,
      said a wary Mrs. Mix.
Could it be that what you need
      is a fishy goldfish kiss?

I think I do, said Ralphie.

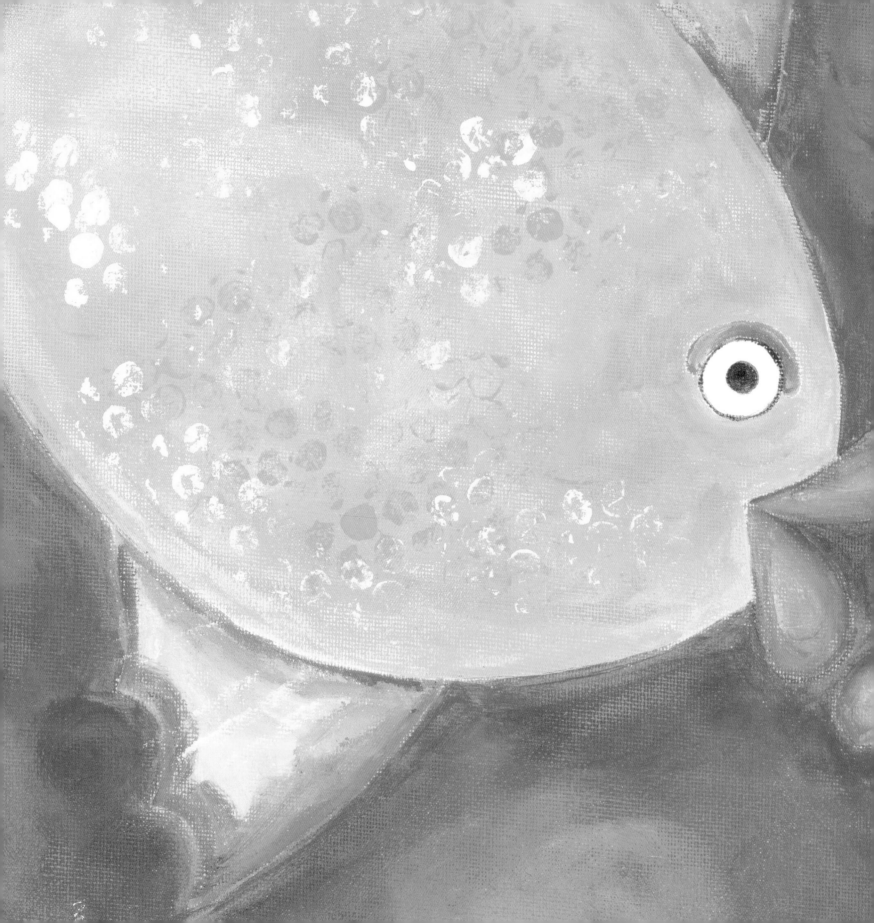

They put their heads together and pulled their cheeks in tight and **KISSED** each other like two fishes looking for a bite.

That's better, said Ralphie.
Good night, Ralphie, said Mom.

Just as Ralphie's mom
    got up to leave his side,
she looked at little Ralphie
    whose eyes were growing wide.

        MOM! said Ralphie,
            I see a monster trying to hide
        behind the closet shelves...
            Oh gosh – he's there inside!

                No monster, Ralphie, said his mom,
                and no bug below your rug.
                    Could it be that what you need
                is one big gorilla hug?

                    I think I do, said Ralphie.

They **WRAPPED** their arms around each other nice and tight and said, "ooh ooh," like mammoth apes using all their might.

ooh oo

...ooh ooh

That's better, said Ralphie.
Good night, Ralphie, said Mom.

Ralphie's mom turned 'round
    to exit from his room,
when Ralphie fell onto the floor
    with a very loud *ka-boom*.

MOM! said Ralphie,
    I see him right out there,
a lion peeking in my window
    and giving me a scare!

Ralphie, said his mom,
    her look growing rather terse.
Your imaginings are growing
    from ridiculous to worse!

There is no bug or lion
    or closet monster, please!
Could it be that what you need
    is a squeezy cobra squeeze?

I think I do, said Ralphie.

They gave each other's belly a strong and lengthy **SQUEEEEZE** as their wiggly giggly hisssssssing brought them to their knees.

That's better, said Ralphie.
Good night, Ralphie, said mom.

Goodness, sighed Ralphie's mom,
about to close the door
when Ralphie Mix, full of tricks,
stayed right there on the floor.

What NOW Ralphie?
        said a flustered Mrs. Mix.
Little boys must get their sleep
        especially at age six!

I hear a loud mosquito, Mom,
   buzzing in my ear.
There he is now, on my ceiling...
   Get him out of here!!

Ralphie, said his mom bemused
   at his talent to befuddle.
Could it be that what you need
   is a cozy polar bear cuddle?

I think I do, said Ralphie.

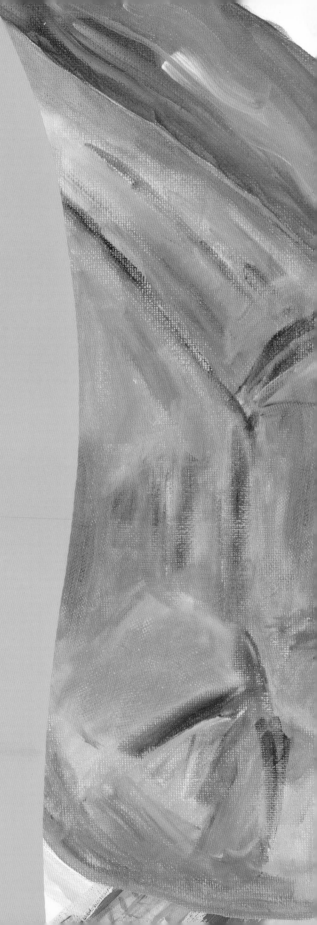

They **HUGGED** like cuddly bears before Ralphie's end of night, growling growly GROOOWWLs as they held each other tight.

That's better, said Ralphie.
Good night, Ralphie, said mom.

Thinking they were done *for sure*,
Ralphie's mom began to leave
when Ralphie said, Oh Mommm?
I need some water, please.

Scared <u>and</u> thirsty? said his mom,
you're being mighty fickle!
Could it be that what you need
is a caterpillar tickle?

I think I do, said Ralphie.

She **TICKLED** Ralphie's tummy, and he **TICKLED** her right back

until the two could laugh no more from the wormy laugh attack.

That's better,
said Ralphie.
Good night, Ralphie,
said mom.

Once and for all, Ralphie's mom
    began to tiptoe down the hall,
hoping not to hear
    the voice that *sure did* call...

Mom?... said Ralphie,
    we forgot to say my prayers,
and you know I cannot sleep
    'til I talk about my cares.

Ralphie's mom came back
   to the edge of Ralphie's bed
and listened to him talk
   about things that filled his head.

Bless mom and dad and grandma
   and my hamster, Butch the 3rd.
Bless all the kids at school…
   and, oh mom, have you heard?

I lost my boots at recess
   and got a pink slip on the bus.
The principal said me and her
   have "issues" to discuss.

But <u>don't worry</u> 'bout it, mom.
   It'll be alright.
In fact, I think it's time
   for me to say goodnight!

No one said a thing just then,
as Ralphie's mom sat still,
holding back her temper
and gathering her will.

Mom? said Ralphie Mix,
   kidding you's a cinch!
Could it be that what you need
   is one rock lobster pinch?

I think I do, said Ralphie's mom.

They **PINCHED** each other's arms up and down with pincer pokes.

Ralphie Mix, laughed Ralphie's mom,
I <u>do</u> not like your jokes!!

Alright Ralphie, said his mom,
 it's time for bed right now.
The night is late, and you must wake
 up for school somehow...

But Ralphie wasn't listening...
 In fact, he didn't make a peep.
Ralphie Mix, at age of six,
 had *finally* fallen asleep!